A Man and His Hat

LETITIA PARR

Clay Animation by Paul Terrett
Photography by Bob Peters

PHILOMEL BOOKS

New York

In memory of Letitia Parr

Text copyright © 1989 by The Letitia Parr Estate
Clay animation copyright © 1989 by Paul Terrett
Photography copyright © 1989 by Bob Peters
All rights reserved. This book, or parts thereof, may not be reproduced
in any form without permission in writing from the publisher.
First American edition published in 1991 by Philomel Books, a division of
The Putnam & Grosset Book Group, 200 Madison Avenue, New York, NY 10016.
Originally published in 1989 by William Collins Pty. Ltd., Sydney. Published simultaneously in Canada
Printed in Hong Kong by South China Printing Company (1988) Ltd.
Library of Congress Cataloging-in-Publication Data
Parr, Letitia.   A man and his hat / by Letitia Parr.   p. cm.
Summary: An old man becomes quite crabby when he cannot find his old shabby hat.
ISBN 0-399-22255-3   (1. Hats—Fiction. 2. Stories in rhyme.)
I. Title.   PZ8.3.P257Man   1991   (E)—dc20   90-35393 CIP AC
First Impression

There was an old man
Who was fond of his hat

It was battered and shabby
But he would get crabby
If searching around
It could not be found.

He'd look all about
And he'd call and he'd shout:

'Just where is my hat?
It was here where I sat,
It was here yesterday.

Did you take it away?
Where's my hat, where's my hat?
It was here where I sat.'

He would rave, he would roar
And go out through the door

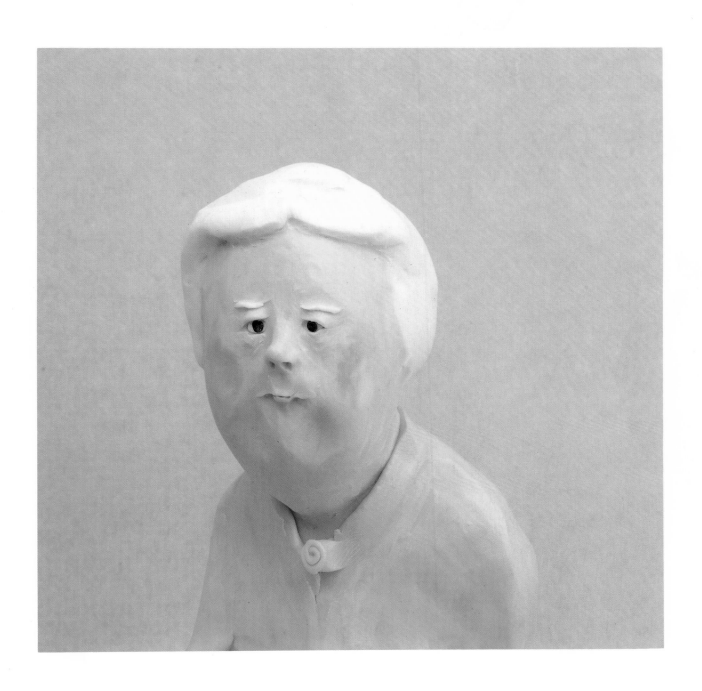

Calling out to his wife
Who was used to such strife:

'I put it just there
Quite close to my chair

When I came in from walking
And we sat there talking.'

Now, his wife was quite nice
So she said to him twice,

'Please calm yourself dear!
Your hat's somewhere here!

I will find it for you,
Don't get into a stew.'

Well, she looked everywhere
Both up and down stairs

But no hat could she find —
Not the old battered kind,

And the man kept on saying,
'I do want my hat

It was here where I sat
Just here near the cat.'

The house-cat was sleeping
All comfy and snug

Curled up like a ball
On the woolly hearthrug.

But the man and his wife
With their clatter and strife

Had disturbed the poor cat
All because of the hat
Which couldn't be found.
It was nowhere around.

Opening one eye, then two
Wondering what next they'd do,

Pussy slowly stretched out
Leaving neither in doubt...

'Look! There is the hat.
Why it's squashed nearly flat!'

Then they pushed at the cat
And they grabbed at the hat...

But the cat did not mind
He knew they were kind.

The man put on his hat
And he patted the cat

And his face changed completely
As he smiled discreetly

And he thanked his dear wife
And said she was nice

Then went out for a walk
Without further talk.

The pussy went too
What else could he do?